I0577622

Other books by Thomas McGonigle

In Patchogue
The Corpse Dream of N. Petkov
Going to Patchogue
St. Patrick's Day: Another Day in Dublin
The Bulgarian Psychiatrist

Published in Bulgarian

Диптих Преди Умиране
  Diptych before Dying

Предсмъртните Видения на Никола Петков
  The Corpse Dream of N. Petkov

PARTY OF PICTURES

THOMAS MCGONIGLE

Mercer
Street
Books

PHOTOS:
Thomas McGonigle
Anna Saar
McGonigle family

To all those who think
and do not think themselves
Irish on St. Patrick's Day

PARTY OF PICTURES

Every year in March there is a *St. Patrick's Day party at *** West 1*ʰ Street. (See note page 132)*

Rarely is it on the actual day, March 17th but it does happen though not this year when it happened on March 11th.

The event was scheduled to start at 1PM in a five-room apartment on the fourth floor. Most of the party occurs in the front sitting room or living room or family room as there has never been an agreement as to what to call this very sunny room overlooking as it does a school yard though because it is on the fourth floor one does not have any sweeping views of Manhattan yet the sense of space created by the open large schoolyard that fronts on Greenwich Avenue gives a pleasant aspect to this room. The windows are blocked for the most part by plants and hanging things—at the moment too complicated to explain—so no one is able to stand at the window and actually look down or out to the beyond.

Half of the people in the room stand or sit with their backs to the windows and the other half is conscious usually of at least the sky behind the people in front of them and sometimes if one is standing one can see slivers of buildings seemingly very far away between the hanging things in front of the windows and the bodies of the people who of course crowd this room, not continuously, but for much of the party, and seated people are often standing up to let another pass or they are standing to move to what might seem like a better seat or to have a conversation or to be left alone for a moment from the burden of conversation as there is sometimes the difficulty of talking with one of the people seen only once during the year and then only at these parties, but since the party only happens once a year, the moment the conversation moves in the direction of going beyond the recent past into either the hopes for the future or, as is more likely, further back into the possibly shared history, a lurch that can bring with it difficulties... as one turns as if to head back into the apartment from this viewing room, one is aware of a long corridor with many closet doors along the left side and on the right one passes a darkened room that is known to be the host's bedroom, then the toilet, then a second bedroom which was most recently occupied by the son of the host and just before we leave the corridor we are aware of one more door to our left that leads to the outside as there are locks along the left side of the door and many pictures of other things and people we are familiar with as we have seen them in other photographs on the walls, taken at many stages of what can only be called The Life, though while the background of these photographs can often identify the occasion of the photo, many are without such distinctions so the viewer is only aware of the movement of time that moves at random via these photographs on the walls and other surfaces in the rooms as there is no chronological order to the photographs though it is true that some of the color photographs reveal their age by the evident chemical changes that attach to the color photographs in a hardly uniform fashion yet mark-

ing them as definitely being from a past further back than some of the other color pictures while at the same time there are black
and white snapshots as they were called, usually much smaller than the 3x4 or the 4x6
which seem to be the most common dimen-
sions of what then must be thought of as
more recent when compared to these surely
older pictures from a time when picture taking was a much more expensive procedure
and usually involved a taking of pictures and
when, as was said, the roll is full, taking that
roll to a photo place to be developed and being given a receipt and an appointed time to
pick up the photographs... however these re-
flections are a consequence of the vast number of pictures in the apartment and do nothing to really describe what one is seeing but
we have continued into another room which
caps the hallway and is designated as the dining room and will contain as it usually does a
very large table covered with various foods.

In the corner right in front as I am entering, I see the "china cabinet" that has been
moved from Brooklyn, to Patchogue, to
Menasha, to Saugerties to here on West 1*th

Street, a rectangular glass-door-fronted dark wood box that contains the china and the glasses that were given to our mother and father at their marriage. These dishes and glasses were only used on "special occasions."

Against the wall to the left is a piano that has not been played for a very long time... though that too was moved from Patchogue, to Menasha, to Saugerties, to here on 1*[th] Street. It collects "stuff"—as in: it *has become a real junk collector*—yet also a place where recent reminders are propped up or little packages of this or that to be given to someone, taken to someone or to be brought to the post office—the top of the piano can not be seen and even the top of the cover that is closed over the out-jutting keyboard serves to hold smaller objects that might easily get lost but which in turn get lost in the haphazard heaping of too many of these things.

Once long ago it had been tuned and for a few times was played by someone my sister knew. It was her piano and she had taken lessons for a long time in Patchogue with a woman who lived over on a small street near the Sandspit—the piano was in the room behind the living room but if one turned to the right one could see the street beyond the porch and to the right an overgrown space of a sort of jungle where if one made one's way through one would be at the Patchogue River, but I believe that my sister never gave herself to such possible adventures which came more naturally or maybe just came to me as I also had to take piano lessons when I was in sixth grade but never got beyond numbering the keys after the fingers which would touch them... combinations of 532... 532... and variations on these numerals as I was incapable of even beginning to master the complicated musical notations on those peculiarly lined pages—as I thought of them—and the teacher did not bother to talk of such but spent time talking about curving my fingers and tapping the keys and not pushing them... or dropping them like so many uncooked hotdogs as she called them, these my fingers... and to keep my feet off the pedals at the base of the piano... but like many things those lessons ended for me after a few months of once-a-week and I think they went on for a much longer period of time for my sister as for the longest time in the bench on which one sat to play the piano the drawer under the lifted up cover of the bench there was a collection of musical pieces—that in truth never appeared when I took lessons—but I assume my sister had used them and worked her way through book after book of these graded musical compositions which for the longest time were collected in the drawer under the seat of the bench on which she had sat but then that also was long over before we had both left Patchogue... yet, the piano continued to be moved.

Turning to the right, away from the piano, one can see a doorway and what is obviously the kitchen beyond this room. Once upon a time a door must have isolated the kitchen but it has long been gone, gone before my sister moved into this apartment. On visits other than for the party, this room is never lit beyond the light coming from the windows that open on a space between the apartment building and the school next door. In its obscurity the kitchen is just that: a place where there is a refrigerator that does not properly close as the door to it has to be propped closed with a five gallon pail of paint on the floor placed as tight as possible against the door. The door has never properly closed and being "too busy with stuff" my sister never complained to the store where she bought it and since the apartment is now owned by my sister and so she is responsible for everything and every condition in the apartment, the refrigerator is something she can live with—if not perfectly—at least it does its job, so one of these days....

The kitchen is small, not modernized as is now very common and the stove and sink are still there from when my sister and other roommates originally moved into this apartment—when it was an ad in the New York Times—now many years ago. There is a near intolerable amount of stuff piled up on the counter next to the sink and on a little table opposite the much soiled stove and on the floor a bit away from the front of the refrigerator bags of stuff to be re-cycled, to be disposed of or awaiting usage... while there are some illustrations taped to the little formerly exposed walls, but by now those scraps of whatever have faded from the assault of the various clouds emanating from the cooking over the years... but by now finally a reasonable person is ready for a drink and the meeting of people, so, reluctantly, the full cataloging of the kitchen will await another time as will the memory of how at one point the kitchen had become so filthy my sister had stopped using it and relied on either delivered meals or eating out. Yet she did use the refrigerator in its various states of neglect as what was she supposed to do?

> a. That was back then. Times change and the whole list of clauses and phrases should be here to indicate the passage of time so we can be present with the first people arriving and we will soon be getting to them.

> b. Yet, we are still caught as if being iron filings drawn across the table by a magnet to again be looking at the public walls of the apartment:

one must exclude my sister's bed room as that door is pushed shut and held there by cascading "stuff" that seems never to arrange itself in proper piles, since as she says, sometimes, she just doesn't have the time and more and more the space into which to sort the years of stuff that continues to collect even at a much diminished rate—but it is the walls with their photographs, drawings, paintings, scraps of newspaper and magazine clippings that formed themselves into panels of hieroglyphics or of some other now "dead" language attached to walls in the British Museum, an allusion to a beginning to the providing of some sort of distance from which to view these rooms and at the same time we are in the home of John

Soane in London though that has acquired a reputation and... of course it is pretentious and a lie to go outside of these rooms here in Eleventh Street when within an obviously limited number of years: all of these walls will be scraped clean, many torn down and not a speck to remind anyone of what had been here before....

c. Though for the moment these walls have always been here and will be for... but the sentences are more secure inside the recent past than of any step into the hours beyond putting these words into the world if to be read only by the person finding this apartment which has not occupied him for some time, though in fact it has been part of his life for more than forty years....

d. Every public wall of the apartment is covered with photographs, drawings, paintings, objects of some sort of personal nature. No one escapes being aware of this aspect once having entered these rooms.

e. In a few places are photographs both large and small of people from *a long time ago* and it can be assumed that these are relatives of the host and possibly of other former tenants of this apartment.

f. What was to appear now is the beginning of a description of these walls and how they were covered and I had walked one time from First Street to Eleventh Street with the intention of taking photographs of these walls and of the room in which they are bound. I had keys for the apartment but at the front door, after ringing the bell two times to be sure my sister was not in or had not loaned the apartment to a friend, I discovered that the front door lock must have been changed. A mother with two young children came to the door and I stepped away, allowing them to enter and not asking to be let in. I tried the keys again and I thought I might obviously be reported for attempting to gain entrance but I had not gained entrance so we can return to the next stage.

g.   (1) I had not wanted to have to rely on my memory of the walls and the pictures I and so many others had seen, as in the comment, your sister's apartment is covered with pictures, and this makes me at first uneasy and then very very sad.

(2) There are four apartments on each floor in this building and all are more or less arranged like this one, though unlike many of these apartments, this one has not been modernized and is pretty much as it was when the host of the party moved into it sometime back in the 1970s.

h. The parties have not been held for that long of a time though she who has always been the host doesn't really remember when she hosted the first party though she is pretty sure she didn't have the parties before the birth of her son who is now on his way to being 33....

i. And the parties began after the death of the father of the father of my sister's child but it is possible that the widow of this man, this rabbi, this distinguished man, was brought to the parties but the host is not that sure of this as it is possible she might or I might be confusing the annual Thanksgiving parties or dinners as those she was (pretty sure) had begun (though they still continue) well before the son was born as that was a neutral sort of holiday not attached to a particular religious tradition.... which was important given the people who might have been involved with her after she met the man who would become the father of her child or *their* child.

j.   Back to—for a moment—the back of the building: not much natural light penetrates from the outside or from the opposite end of a corridor to the dining room which is located in front of the kitchen which is seen as the back room of this apartment, the back wall of which is behind the back wall of the apartment in front of this one which overlooks West 11th Street, though to be scrupulous, both of these back walls are separated by the vertical tunnel for the elevator. I have never been in this other apartment and all these years I have only been in the apartment across from the one where these words are being found and yes, I have been in one other apartment but that is very vague and I don't remember the occasion though it was surely an occasion neither notably happy nor sad as those are the extremes that often attach themselves to places seen only once or twice... but if there was no such dimension: the place can't exist beyond the possibility that in more than thirty years, surely, I had to have been in another apartment other than the one across the hall and which was known as a widow's apartment, a woman who had survived the death of her husband by many years and this apartment had been sold by the owners of the building to someone who would never live in the apartment but hold it as an investment which would pay off once this woman was dead and gone, remembered only by my sister and who else....

Another way to enter into the spirit of this day's party and all the parties from the many previous years shadowing each and every one of the people who walk about in these rooms:

some are waiting for the moment when they can leave without drawing attention to their leaving and others are waiting finally to talk for long moments with a person who seems so busy all the time, and then there are those people who seem to be props—if this can be said without demeaning or making less of these participants in this day's activities as so many of these people are essential and have long attended this party without making a distinctive defining memorable contribution to the accumulated fact of this event, a simple one at that: it is that time of the year for the host's St. Patrick's Day party and while a few people, who for a long time were both active and passive participants in the party, will not be there, it is hoped that not too much will be made of their not being in attendance as they are either scattered ash or entombed rotting flesh... though some are not in attendance due to more mundane circumstances: illness, the demands of necessary travel to a far or near place, an argument someone might have had with one of the regulars and with no way to recapture the spent words or ease them into polite understanding, and finally a few just will have forgotten in spite of the written and mailed invitation together with the follow up electronic reminder and possibly even a phone call which usually in this day is recorded on some sort of answering device, just to be forgotten it would seem in the rush of events.

However, there must be asserted the urgent rewinding of the imaginary film—if that is a convenient way for a reader to understand, some of the necessary and preliminary steps in the re-creation of this St. Patrick's Day party. It would seem obvious a person might ask where was all of this taking place?

It is true we have begun to see an apartment appear and aspects of it have been presented... but did anyone unsure of such things ask where in exactly what country, what city, on what street and in which building on that street as surely this apartment was not in a building existing in a sort of splendid isolation with even a possible moat surrounding it...? though in mind one might have thought of the office building remains in the images of the aftermath of the Hiroshima bombing or the remains of the Kaiser Wilhelm Memorial church at the head the Kurfurstendamm —that is, thoughts of a certain disposition which allow one to walk about and to exist in a constant shadow of...(here should be left blank as any word that would complete the phrase might give a very false impression or a possibly too accurate aspect of the person recording this event.)

However, on the contrary, the building in which the apartment is located is next to the school on West Eleventh Street in "The Village" between Sixth and Seventh Avenue. At one time long before anyone now living in the building or even visiting the building, there was likely to have been a doorman and possibly even an elevator operator and all that remains of this possible moment is the name of the building

UNADILLA

which is displayed embedded in the tiled entranceway which is smartly elegant to a certain extent... but on such a day as this party only someone who had planned to meet someone before going up to the party together would have lingered in the doorway before the first door to the side of which is a directory of names and the apartment numbers which are to be pressed to hear a question as to who is ringing the bell and that person is directed to enter the door and proceed to the next door and ring the desired apartment for a second time and hearing the buzzing sound in the door one walks in and then along the length of the brightly lit hallway toward the back of the building where the elevator is to the left while there is a staircase to the floors above to one's right.

Escaping the moment of this walking and then waiting for the elevator to appear, the years come back as to the sometime unreliability of the elevator and so the ease, back then, of walking up the flights of stairs to the fourth floor... rather than to wait for the arrival of the elevator which often would descend rather than ascend as someone had pushed the button in the basement summoning the elevator to that destination and often the elevator would have to stop again on the ground floor during its new ascent....

Obviously, it can be noticed a certain reluctance to go up to the party, and this would be

an accurate reading as the person recording
this moment has to confess:

A CONFESSION

I am not sure when I first came to this apartment
to visit the hostess of today's party who was then
living in these rooms with two other women and
a man... it could be as long ago as late in 1974
when Europe was exhausted by me and I had to
return to the United States and there was even an
incident on the plane when I opened the
Beefeater gin to have a private drink and I was
told by the suddenly appearing air marshal as they
were then called to close the bottle and put it in
the overhead luggage and if it was seen to be
taken down again it would be confiscated.

That evening the bottle of gin appeared in
the apartment upstairs and upon the hostess's
return from her work it was then consumed
mostly by myself as the three women and
man did not drink gin.

If the year of this event was identified with
either a reference to a public event or to the
actual year itself, that information might discourage further reading of these pages since it
would seem then to have now more a historical interest as in *a raking up of those ashes* than

the sort of interest prose of the nature you have been reading wishes to create which is to root the reader in the present moment of his or her reading without the tedious insertion of this event into the ever moving revolving moment with its inevitable degradation into some things called: the present, the past, the future.

The appearance of a photograph insists upon some sort of explanation, as the reader is suddenly being asked to recall Henry James allowing for photographs to appear in the "New York Edition" of his collected work.

However, the reader has to understand (one hopes this aspect of the writing being read will not hinder this person): the part of Eleventh Street where this building is located is associated in my and in many another's memory with the appearance of certain writers whose names are known: Nelida Pinon, Thomas Pynchon, Donald Barthelme, Grace Paley, S.J. Pearlman, and W.S. Trow... as well as with (at the corner) the hospital that is no longer there, having accommodated the death of Dylan Thomas and the life of the person transcribing this text from imagination who found himself in this hospital on a number of occasions and one can reasonably expect a re-counting of some of these stays and visits even as the party upstairs is calling urgently to return to the stepping out of the elevator on the fourth floor, and as the door of that con-veyance closes there, to the going to the left and finding at the end of a short hall two doors and our destination is again on the left.

The door is a bit ajar since we are not the first to arrive from the noise appearing (as it were), as the door opens with a gentle push and an almost inevitable resistance as obviously a shoulder of someone or other has hindered the door from fully opening and, while the door is moving, a long chain of bright shiny plastic shamrocks—extending in a diagonal fashion across the door bisecting the spy hole in the center of the door—moves in a pleasant anonymous sort of welcome, it could be said... though upon thought and that is what happens within a recounting of such an event, the event, since it has recurred for so many years, does not urge promptness of attendance upon anyone beyond the hostess, who also now finds herself taking more and more time with the preparations for the party during a period of time that begins just after New Year's Day when she opens one of the gift calendars and begins to enter information in some of the demarcated spaces for each of the oncoming days: dates not to be forgotten and dates for which she must make plans far ahead of time as is the St. Patrick's Day party... but this entering of information on a calendar is not only an incident for the hostess since many of the guests will also be marking their calendars when they receive the invitation in the mail, and as I have done, some even insert them in their diaries that are also prepared for the oncoming year and the soon enough departing year... much as this party on this day will soon be over and we will be coming out of the door we are entering yet we will not be looking at the outside of the door as we leave beyond the possible glance from the so-called corner of the eye as we turn to the right in our leaving the apartment hearing the door close, not with a slamming sound but with the sense of sudden severing of our connection with the noise of conversations continuing even after we have left, which for a moment seems strange as it crosses my mind, surely they have nothing more to say to each other now that I have left—thus confirming an aspect of a monstrous egotism they—who is this *they?*—have attached to me, the brother of the hostess, *but how has she!* —with the hard

sound of an imaginary exclamation point appearing between pronoun and quickly enunciated verb—*put up with him all these years but then
it is just the two of them... and didn't he live in this
apartment on the sofa for some time, way back* and a
head might nod in the memory but for most
of the remaining guests it is safe to say that
they think the hostess did arrive in this apartment and that is the setting for the life they
understand as her own and whatever came
before it might be in the few scattered black
and white photographs on the walls, but some
of those pictures are mixed with the history
of the father of her child and come to think
of it with this thought about any possible
confusion as to whose childhood was being
remembered in these photographs: we do
know the brother who has now left would be
very annoyed and would not resist mentioning his dislike of this confusion because
wasn't it obvious whose family was being depicted...? And such a rhetorical question
makes everyone uncomfortable but a few are
aware that he enjoys that aspect of such a
question.

Yet, everyone knows there is a limited interest in matters of such intimacy—an intimacy that does not hint at perversity—if such a thing any longer exists—but it is just too personal, like, as they say, having to ask a person if they brushed their teeth this morning? That terrible word *like*! which embodies the collapse of conversation within its four letters. Yet this linguistic flaw lurches the prose away from and now to: the description of any event is always difficult beginning with such a depressing, frequently and probably useless repetitive admission, so now the very opening of the sentence can take on the intimidatingly comic or grotesque "what?" (or not) or is it verbal throat clearing?—thus as to say: The Rabbi has appeared and of course now it seems appropriate to begin the description of the party with a person who is in fact——whatever that can mean?—not in the room and cannot in any drearily realistic sense be so since he is permanently restrained by six feet of earth and the metal of the box in which he remains—yet still: The Rabbi is in the room. You can see him in photographs on the wall. Sadly, some of them are bursting into unrecognizable shapes of color because

of the temporary nature of color photogra-
phy of a certain moment some years ago.

Yet, this is a distraction of a distraction,
you could say or a foreboding distraction to
the well aware.

A person enters the apartment though the
door fortunately does not slam behind this
person as a slamming door has a terrible reputation, nearly as foreboding as the gun appearing in the first act of a play and having to
be fired by the third act, just as surely the
door must on occasion slam shut near the
end of the party and probably given the nature of some of the inhabitants of the party,
it can be said, a slamming of the door will oc-
cur on more than one occasion when the
thoughtful and the listening will note the moment and will catalog the provocations that
are capable of such a final gesture, a gesture
beyond words and while not as word-provok-
ing as a suicide, there will be no avoiding the
comments and the near relative: the commentary....

So, the Rabbi is now in residence, and it is
of the moment for his wife to appear and she
is always to be addressed as **Rose, please,**

Rose will do as it has done for me all these years but no Rosy as that is not to my liking or personality.

Her title: Rose the Rebbetzin, please to stand or sit on that formality, she might give a wave as to... dismiss this from her presence though by doing so one is always aware, as one is of the absence of the Rabbi who was together in many of the previous years here with Rose, please Rose, we don't want to hear that again, he might be saying and she would say, you have been saying that for a long time and I will say what has to be said... but the simple fact of his disappearance and her con-tinued appearance was long noted and then no longer noted, as life just goes on as we all know, dumbly without our consent and there will be a year when **she is not here** and an-other year when she will be here and one is hearing her say, I feel jolly for some reason, said with a sort of English accent by way of Second Avenue in Manhattan—was it not called the Jewish Rialto—where they screen —so long ago that wedding movie in Yiddish though did she speak or was she told to move her lips but to allow nothing to come out as that was the best role for a woman of her sort, to speak but not a sound to be heard, which was a remembered comment together with the understanding, I guess could be said, that such activities could not continue in her marriage to The Rabbi whose position would not allow for her to follow such a life....

Yet on this last visit, could it be really that? are you sure?—as I remember another time, but you could be right or wrong of course, really, now Rose says, I'd like my drink please, I feel jolly and quick about it, please....

HOWEVER, there is the nagging reality of being stuck as it were in the entranceway just as the door is about to slam shut when it is pushed as if to allow a newly arriving guest entrance to the party and I or you have turned our back and are moving to the left as one enters just for a moment, to be sure to say Hello to the hostess who is arranging platters of something or other to be taken to the front room, and being careful not to slip, to fall, to knock the platter against the wall: to arrive safely in the front room and deposit the platter or something or other on the low table in the middle of the room.

Still, entering is a something that can only be said to be forecast as having happened within the rather immediate experiences of everyone concerned and at the same time all of these people will be unaware of the complicated figuring that goes into the simple, possibly too simple entering into a familiar apartment, familiar because of that old fashioned thing: blood relations... yet there is another something or other which allows for the so-called living and the so-called dead to be ever present, even with the Rabbi's objections.

However, confusion suddenly arouses the ear to hearing questions: **WHAT TIME IS IT? DOES ANYONE KNOW ANYTHING ABOUT THE TIME...?** the sound of turning heads—disguised except to those hearing with ears attached to heads upon arthritic necks as the blood pushes against enlarging diseased bone tissue, glasses being dropped from the hand, a bottle falling out of hand and shattering contrary to the description in small print at the bottom of the back of the front label: shatter proof bottle....

Hours later....

No way can you escape what came next and next and next. You are here for the duration, don't worry, it is not as bad or as easy as a wisdom teeth extraction: come to think of it has anyone correlated the decline in an individual's IQ with the removal of the wisdom teeth?

The party can be said to be almost in full swing and will continue in that state for a few more hours when the first departures are announced and the first regrets tendered, received and stabbed into the departing backs with some traditional departing words: don't let the door hit you on your heels, as the insurance has not been paid and ain't no money in the piggybank for the likes of yourself with your carping criticism of the... what was it... no matter, as forgettable as your presence, though didn't that guy say something about a failure of nerve on the part of someone or other at this or that, what was it, do you remember and hearing got me there, it all passes through one ear and out the other as we used to say when a kid would bring a flashlight to school and holding it up to this guy's ear, saying, I can see right through, but to a confirmation of the dreariness of the ***moment in time***, as is said, no one dared confront the statement with the obvious suggesting of turning out the lights to see if the light really did come through that guy's head with not being stopped by any brain-matter what-so-ever.

The lights will not go out. The sunshine will dim as the day wears on. Weather will only be within the past and future tenses.

The hostess for this party just doesn't have time to talk immediately to each and every person who she has invited to the party. It is true she also sees many of these people during the course of her passing months yet some *dear* (old)[1] *friends* who she only sees at this occasion are especially understanding though everyone knows at some time during the party she will talk to them in an immediate rush of what has been happening, what is going to happen and what has happened to this or that one and when are we ever to get

---

1   The word "old" is not said and is here inserted but should not be said out loud since the passage of time is not to be so under-lined

together as we once did, do you remember and of course the heads both nod as the hostess sharply turns away as if smacked across the face with the sudden urgency of having to return to the kitchen as some of the food is still cooking and there are bottles still immediately to be opened for which she passes the opener to... and this person takes up the implement and opening the bottle presents it to the hostess and she gives it back to him suggesting always suggesting he find a place he thinks suitable for... while taking the opening instrument and giving it to another to take care of the opening of another bottle that is not to be placed near the one just opened, please, she says, see if you can find a good place for it.

(The word *screw* was avoided in the previous paragraph since it was thought to be incitement to unpleasant sexual insinuations.)

Fortunately for all concerned no music is being played on the various machines in the front room... we have only the music of the human voice... is heard to be said, but no person can be connected to this sentiment; immediately as always lurking is the possibility of a conversation taking up which opera has recently been seen...

      ... or is it heard?—that is one of those byways to such an opening gambit, outwardly innocent, as to which opera has been recently heard, though if a person asks which opera have you been to see... can it not lead to a possible discussion of which is the better approach to opera: does one see an opera or does one hear an opera though often if a person has been subjected to this complex question as to whether one has seen or heard an opera this person might say I was at the opera last night— and while there are occasional opera matinees, the attendance at such might provoke the most delicate of condescending expressions an eyebrow is capable of... yet we have been spared the movements of a face offering either approval or disapproval since the person about whom an opera can be said to swirl has not yet appeared or he has not been seen or heard but surely he will be in attendance as he has been at attendance in some fashion to the hostess for forty years and counting, or not counting, as counting can have a tendency to be what used to be called *a downer* and while, when he is about, he is not talked about since that can lead a conversation in directions....

Let us leave this sentence to dangle... as surely what is right in front of the eyes is of such a complex interest there is required a violent swerve away from this beating about the bush, which is a complex metaphor to say the least, and yet that is what has been happening for the very simple reason no one has asked why does this party happen every year and while it shall not survive the eventual oblivion of the hostess it will be recalled by her relatives and friends who in turn might have passed along mentionings of this party always happening in the month of March... but as we are all given to some interest in the future one finally wonders what will be remembered of these hours which maybe have already disappeared along with the hours that went into the preparation for that hour... such melancholic thoughts are rushed through, one might say, with the speed of a fast forward on whichever electronic device one might like to allude to, aware of course that whichever one named, it will eventually date this telling providing ever a charming reminder of the recent quickly vanishing past or a dating detail to allow a

certain attitude of superiority that always is an at-
tribute of anyone who has survived into the future glad to be done with all of that, whatever *that*
might have been.

Called to the senses, the eyes wander about
the walls again in the front room, noticing recent
additions to the representations of the captured
souls as they used to be referred to in one sort of
dated literature. These images are never of the
aging but of the recent arrivals who having been
put on the very beginning of the chute have begun their inevitable sloping voyage into....

The tale continues, as it must, turning from

the glare of sun-light and entering once again the long hall in the direction of the cooking, the heaping up of the various foods to be consumed in that room just before the kitchen... there is a voice saying, we are all here for a very happy occasion... there is a voice saying, we're all here for a very happy occasion, there's a voice saying, we're all here for a very happy occasion: it is as if... no, it can't be a voice being passed along in the move to the rear of the apartment from one mouth to another though there is the same intonation, the same absence of any response, no matter the slight variation which was indi-cated by the appearance of an apostrophe... so possibly there is no accounting for this sentiment being stated which was still within the ear at the arrival in the center of the building while looking into the kitchen and meeting the hostess returning a look to the person entering the room: where have you been, no matter, don't tell me, or tell me later, we have so much that needs to be done....

Startled could be the unspoken response, realizing she has not registered in any way that this is a day which has been declared to be a day for a happy occasion. And out of the silence of our reply we have returned—in an imagined impersonation of the Papal first-person plural and in hearing the doing so—to the hostess asking for some help in the carving of the various meats to be offered to the hungry—I do hope everybody has brought their appetites to this party as I don't want to be responsible for housing any left-overs. No one should feel they have to eat dead animal as we have many other options, so many in fact, but I need help now!

A new element was introduced without being immediately acknowledged by the friends gathered in this party—the suppression of the word *guest* was obvious as it had become so current in every five-dollar motel on the road: *stop in and be treated as a guest* not as a customer or mere number.

There is no rush to aid the hostess and while rooted in the adjacent room one is possessed by a feeling... the sense of duty comes to the fore—the crudeness of a remembered: get the lead out, will you, enough of this dancing on the head of needle or is it spinning your angels on the head of a needle, without wondering why not the more difficult task of spinning the angels or the self on the point of the needle?

So, what can I do?

Ham or tongue are offered with the beef tongue being immediately placed by the hostess, direct from one of the two large pans on the stove, onto the carving dish as we'll allow the little guy to do the ham since he likes the Kosher part of the pig, as he says and laughs at his making this religious distinction in the meats to be on offer.

The tongue came from a beef, as no one really wants to say the word cow as that might bring to the fore maternal feelings in the hostess or some of the other sensitive souls in attendance....

But there is a compulsion to mention that the last place in Manhattan where you could easily get a tongue sandwich was in the garment district, but only in or near those streets where the fur merchants were and it was always said that the guys who worked in the fur trade liked to have a tongue sandwich... and it was a featured sandwich in the delis... but with the passage of years, the ruthless passage of years to emphasize the nature of change in New York City, if it even has to be so exaggerated, but allow that to pass... here we are watching a tongue from the side as the outer skin has to be removed... the pebbly sort of layer which must contain the taste-buds, and it has never been argued that this is a delicacy not to be missed... even by those know-it-alls that always populate any party or larger gathering in New York City: equaled only by the experts on opera who compete with the gourmets in that rather elevated circus of always knowing a great deal about either food or opera and the masses—that herd of consumers are just so many cows in their ignorance... to be beaten, as actors were said to be by that film master Alfred Hitchcock....

The outer layer is cut away and then the tongue is set up as if to stick out of the mouth of a beef cow without the upper and lower jaws framing this anatomy... and these ovals of tongue are arranged on the platter and it is suggested ketchup should be provided on a little saucer so the hostess has done this together with the hot Coleman's mustard that must be prepared in a small cup by mixing powder and water while the hostess is always saying year after year, it gets harder each year to find the tongue and the mustard powder but that is what Dad always liked... the hot mustard....

The verbal insertion of the admittance of a personal past is quite unusual on the part of the hostess who rarely mentions her personal past so each of such mentions will be recorded in a sort of incomplete anti-thesis to the walls that constantly urge a deep swim into the immediate and distant pasts as, in the eyes of the guests, can be seen a constant of both staring and an avoiding the staring at the photographic reminders of their previous selves.

But now each guest has remembered where those personal reminders are and one would not have to be *that*... to notice the sudden turning of a head, a lowering of eyes at the appearance on the wall of that moment... and not everyone who wanders about the apartment midst the party is so favored by a fragmented photographic time line sending them to this very moment in this year's gathering— a way to avoid saying *party* as there will be no communal singing, no exchanging of presents or even the giving over of those offerings some insist on always bringing as the hostess has strictly forbidden any such as she does not wish to send thank-you notes or deal with the on-going guilt of not having sent the thank-you notes in a timely manner....

Yet, it is this eye and head movement that is of real interest, beyond the ephemeral nature of a guilt that can be associated with an act of a tardy thank-you note, towards those so favored or burdened with reminders of: the very far past or the more recent past or finally the immediate past. It is easy to observe that reminders of the very distant past have no instantaneously contemporary thoughts of a deeply disturbing nature while those which recall the immediate past or the not too distant past are causes of various and throughout the party immediate distressing feelings which for some allow for the consumption of excessive alcohol-laced drinks or for others the eating of too much... and for others thoughts that make inviting the idea: let's go up on the roof and see who can hang over the edge the furthest?

However, in spite of this sudden curlicue of possible despair, the party is underway, swimmingly, to use an adverb once within fashion but now hinting at a memory of bee-hive hairdos and the crazy things we did as kids, can even be heard as....

At the same time a second tongue has been fetched from the large pan by the hostess and again it is being carved... *a man's job* is an ironic comment that is said and no one contradicts it, though in the sudden comings and goings in the room where the "feast" is to be laid out, there is the possibility that the remark was not heard or if heard fell on non-confrontational ears... for what is the point in this day of the age of such a comment except the ironic referencing that the hostess was participating in?

During the statement about the thinking, a second platter has been filled with tongue and the other fellow who was doing the ham has filled his platter and so we are about to go, the hostess is heard to say, and she is asking people to begin to come and fill their plates, as I want no leftovers.

The dog is dead and I don't have any of

those Styrofoam boxes... at the mentioning of *the dog* some of the guests supplied the name of the dog, **Lightning**, remembering it was a husky with a marking of a lightning bolt on its forehead and it was appreciated that there was not a twin for this bolt of lightning so the Second World War would not have to be discussed due to the referencing of the German SS via the twin lightning bolt insignia... by the singular lightning bolt the Second World War would not immediately be called into the present moment, to much relief as they wanted to talk about what happened when they took the subway, was it or the bus, was it, or did they actually take the train out to The Island and no one asked do you mean Staten Island as there is only one island ever referred to when it is said, out To The Island.

As messengers are being sent by the hostess to the front room bearing the command to come and fill your plates while the food is hot, *a guest and his partner*.... Oh, another will say, Kevin, you mean? and heads will nod... and a quick and thorough glance is made to be sure there is a sufficient human barrier between the one looking and this Kevin....

But our interest must for some moments be with this late arriving guest who had to come all the way down from what is referred to as The Orange House... in Upstate New York.

The guest and Kevin no longer drive into the city. They have taken the train and the sentences about that experience are sure to be repeated at a later moment by one of the two so they can be postponed to yet another, and for sure it will be said again as there are some essential details that must be here disclosed about this guest and Kevin.

This guest used to be, a long time ago, a resident of this apartment and then at a later date he found an apartment further along on 11th Street on the other side of Seventh Avenue but that apartment has now been sold and this guest lives upstate in The Orange House.

This Orange House has never had the guest's name attached to it as is so easily done in other situations when one hears: that is my wife's house, or my brother-in-law's house or my parent's house... this guest does not like to own things or at least demonstrate what he thinks is a vulgar expression of proprietorship revealed by the attaching his name to The Orange House.

And for all the years of the hostess's knowing of this guest, she has never attached his name to The Orange House and in accord with that revelatory practice his name will never be disclosed though it should also be known that he has known the hostess in what used to be known as having had a carnal knowledge of her, and a child was the result of this intense something—at least then it was, for a few moments—and as is also said: a few moments and a lifetime to live with the consequences in the form of at first a baby, then a child and now an adult who has not arrived as of yet to the party since he too comes with a wife, the mother of their child, which can be said accounts for both his now tardy arrival and the occasional facial expressions of anxiety on the face of the hostess which she will conceal by asking if everything is all right to whomever is standing in front of her.

Some may say that there is in the language of these two arrivals an odd formality along with an obvious intimacy that takes the form of an oppressive need to constantly express an immediate interest in whatever sentence has come from a person's mouth and usually this interest is shaped in an extreme positive viewpoint, so far in that direction that a person of a skeptical nature might decide there was a purposeful comic aim in the background waiting for a target as wide as the Mississippi which is not to say that there are other rivers which might be wider but sometimes an immediate access to a familiar place can be recommended as long as in this case we do not want to linger too long on the word *Mississippi* as they might call up both the experience of the guest and by inference Kevin and, even more extreme, the example set by both this guest and the Rebbe, as the father of the guest, who it must also be mentioned would not provide a reliable commentary on—here quote marks are provided with a pantomime of fingers resident in both the right and left hand of the listener—"the relationship" of the guest to Kevin.

In interest of curtailing any suspense: both the guest and the Rabbi had been politically interested and to some extent involved themselves in **the movement**—and of course you do not need a nudge as to what movement was being referenced—but if you wanted to be sure there will be ample time to hear of it in due course as the party moves its way through the various courses within the food service.

No attempt is being made to postpone political discussion, but it is sometimes better to take up "**the movement**" when the stomachs of the various participants in the likely discussion and its inevitable course will have eaten their fill—though they would all reject the very concept that a person can ever be filled or "satisfied" since that implied a limit to the imagination and in one voice they give rise to the refrain:

TO BE SATISFIED IS TO DIE

A change in the projected course of this conversation is urged upon the few by an even fewer number who are turning to remember the father of the guest in another

of his roles: the Rebbe was a rabbi on se-
lected cruise lines that moved about "the islands" and even ventured to the Pacific on
occasion when the destination port was
Acapulco....

This being a rather chilly day for this annual
holiday celebration it seems obvious why a few
would rather be taken with moving among
"the islands" where one did not need to worry
so much about keeping warm though no one
should make light of just how difficult it was
for all who traveled in the party of a rabbi on
these cruises to select clothing suitable for
their various supporting roles.

Of course, there was the wife of the rabbi,
plus the guest who remains un-named and the
hostess who was with child on one of these
cruises. While easy to overlook in the big
scheme of things, a brother and sister of the
guest had to be mentioned as being members
of the rabbi's party—how he would like not
to think of this group as a party since that
gave a wrong tone to his presence on these
ships—but he thought it essential for himself
as the spiritual resource on the ship, to be
seen as a model of decorum, and his family

along to bear witness to it. A more objective eye would note that the article *the* should be corrected to the humble *a* as a Catholic priest and Protestant minister of an undefined subset of that spiritual division were also accommodated to provide their own particular councils to the members of their flocks—or congregations, depending on the home base usage.

The rabbi had an expansive definition of family so as to include the then pregnant hostess who was while not in that dreary legalism wedded to the guest not named, had been impregnated by this man in the rather conventional manner of the time though mentally supported by approximately only ten percent of his sexual drive—we will draw a curtain across how he reveled behind it for the remaining ninety percent.

The rabbi did draw a rather arbitrary line against the companion of his daughter who came complete with a much older "friend"— a woman some might say who was nearly as old as her mother yet the two together were known to make rather flamboyant displays of their affections in a way Queen Victoria was not allowed to even contemplate....

Please. Please. The pleasure of recalling the recent and the far away past can not be allowed to interfere too much in the fact: we have only this day which is being occupied, by many people within these walls, with having a good time, really.

This is a party and we must move along as there seems to be a movement of people in the front room to make room for... a psychiatrist who bestowed his children like flowers midst the crowd both to entertain, if you like such an entertainment, or as an annoyance since this was the more usual result. The four, as distinctive as grains of wheat, were particular favorites of the hostess and she, stepping into the 19th Century, *bustled* about making them comfortable with the sheets of paper, little chairs and a table that seem to appear as if by magic in a space cluttered to the roof, to use a cliché, yet there it was: four children recreating a masterpiece from the world of art and receiving with a certain assurance the approval of the guests.

The hostess left having clapped three distinct yet discreet times at: have you noticed how well behaved the children are?

Of course, one wants to agree and it is a miracle how this table, these off-spring of the psychiatrist and his wife (who have immediately left the room to have a moment free of these products of at least four sexual encounters with each other) are now present midst the crowd of people who moved aside for this imposition—if one was unkindly inclined —or a welcome addition to this gathering of us old folk; and the immediate rejoinder: who are these old people you are including?—and slowly, ever so slowly, the room seems to grow silent as the number of adults melts away into other parts....

As in the old Westerns when a person is said to have lit out for a far country... **a pause.** The film is caught, there is danger...,

... AN INTRUSION.

A NECESSARY TAKING OF THE ROLL AS TO WHO WAS IN ATTENDANCE AT THE PARTY. It was clearly visible that the rooms had rabidly filled and soon enough no one could keep track of who was who so a brief listing of the guests is called forth and as might echo the gospel: and a petition went out that each was to go to his hometown and register... something along those lines... a census was it... in what age... well, right now: NOTE... readers are allowed to skip along to the text without fully digesting this listing which is here to reassure... it is also not as complete as it should be...

THE HOSTESS
THE GUEST
KEVIN
THE RABBI
THE WIFE OF THE RABBI
THE BROTHER OF THE
    HOSTESS
THE WIFE OF THE BROTHER
    OF THE HOSTESS
THE SON OF THE HOSTESS
THE WIFE OF THE SON OF THE
    HOSTESS
THE CHILD OF THE SON OF
    THE HOSTESS AND HIS
    WIFE

DAWSON
THE WIFE OF DAWSON
THE DAUGHTER OF DAWSON
        AND HIS WIFE
THE HUSBAND OF THE
          DAUGHTER OF DAWSON
          AND HIS WIFE
THE SON OF DAWSON AND HIS
          WIFE
THE WIFE OF THE SON OF
          DAWSON AND HIS WIFE
THE UPSTAIRS NEIGHBOR
THE "FRIEND" OF THE
          UPSTAIRS NEIGHBOR
THE DEAD HUSBAND OF THE
WOMAN WHO WAS THE
BEST FRIEND OF THE
HOSTESS
THE WOMAN WHO WAS THE
          BEST FRIEND OF THE
          HOSTESS
THE BROTHER OF THE GUEST
THE SISTER OF THE GUEST
THE BUTTERFLY MAN
THE WIFE OF THE BUTTERFLY
          MAN

THE PSYCHIATRIST
THE WIFE OF THE
          PSYCHIATRIST
THE FOUR CHILDREN OF THE
PSYCHIATRIST
THE FORMER WIFE OF THE
          BROTHER OF THE
          HOSTESS
THE IRISH FRIEND OF THE
          FORMER WIFE OF THE
          BROTHER OF THE
          HOSTESS AND IS ALSO
          THE   FRIEND OF THE
          BROTHER OF THE
          HOSTESS
MIMI
AND A CAST OF TENS....

The hostess has scurried in her fashion back to the room where people are *digging in* and as she appears—a plate drops from the hands of the butterfly man who stands eyes staring as if contemplating the pattern the food and paper plate have created and in the hesitation someone asks him if he is still offering tours of the butterflies in the museum?

The butterflies have gone undescribed for a few weeks, he is heard to say, as I have had to attend to the needs of the water pipes of the place Upstate... but do you see how the food separated from the plate upon contact with the floor?

There is no reply to this aesthetic observation by anyone in the immediate presence of this action and the resulting commentary— the pause suddenly interrupted by the wife of the butterfly man who asks with a distinct rhetorical flourish, is my husband going to clean up after himself?

The hostess chooses not to get involved in this eddy of something she is not interested in because it is so obvious that there are guests who are not eating, not preparing to eat or who have finished eating and wondering what they are supposed to do with the freedom of now having eaten, a doubt etching lines of anxiety into the lips of certain guests and with others one can only conclude they are just pausing waiting for the next course to make its appearance on the table though a twitch of irritability can be detected and the hostess has a built-in device

—anatomical location undisclosed—for recognizing such slight turns which demand an immediate correction as such can undermine the carefully hoped for conclusion to this yearly gathering, and when people are preparing to hear: what a wonderful year to look forward to as again next year we shall all be gathered in these rooms... the hostess has not time to pause to acknowledge her astute defusing of the possible irritability except by: **could you** help me clear the used silverware which was our mother's, she turns saying in the direction of her brother who knows he will now be hearing about the time a certain young woman was invited to 41 Furman Lane for Sunday dinner and he had requested his mother, our mother in the hostess's formulation, to bring out the real silver from the wooden box that only appeared twice a year: Christmas and Thanksgiving.

Imagine, HE WANTED to have this silver on the table when that girl came for dinner—a dinner at 3PM, much later than we ever had it back then—and he had always complained on these two annual holidays of how heavy and uncomfortable the actual silver was to use and always insisted on using the ordinary kitchen silverware that was made from some sort of base metal....

Our mother had to polish the silver, and he didn't ask to help her though they both knew she would not allow either of them to polish the silver as that was one of the roles a wife was meant to have in the house. This was something she had learned up in Newburgh where she summered with relatives... and they had a lot of silver that had to be cleaned even though it was never used.

People had standards up in Newburgh, our mother used to say, the hostess saying—un-aware that only one person at the party other than the hostess's brother had once upon a time had the possibility of meeting this woman—an awkward intrusion to be sure—then known as *this is my mother*

(allow a pause)

as a family we would go up to Newburgh from Patchogue back then for weddings and funerals.

Of course much later my brother would go on about that conjunction of events and what they meant to our sense of growing up: you got married and you died.

Now it may be asked if this digression was actually based on an incident observed in this party, at this moment?

A Confession is ordered—non-religiously specific—and apologies for a possible insertion of an allusion to a sacrament of the Roman Catholic Church.

Sometimes, in the course of this party, time has a tendency to get jumbled about as if suddenly the hitherto flight to......... was suddenly battered with head winds and with seat belts fastened and which moment is the plane going to fall apart? But as soon as it begins we are back walking the aisles, preventing blood clots....

Just put the dirty silverware in the kitchen sink, the hostess orders the dithering—what a nice adjective someone is heard to say—Dawson who having been given the order reaches out to pick up the nearest silverware and is rebuked by the hostess, I said the *dirty* silverware... please, and Dawson, as a man used to being told what to do, places each of the unused spoons that he finds himself holding one next to the other on the table, and the hostess does conceal her annoyance as she simply pushes them together so as to make room for the coffee cups that make their appearance as there are always a few who require coffee at some point in the proceedings....

The wife who is thought to be the best friend of the hostess and whose husband died some years ago—it was remarked in passing how much he looked forward to these parties, even if he was of Italian origin, since Columbus Day had become an occasion for controversy—was trying to answer a question which was both a challenge and provocation from the so-called boyfriend of the unnamed: is it possible to celebrate in a secular fashion a day named for what in one of the particular branches of the Christian belief system was labeled, in their peculiar hierarchical jargon: a saint?

The hostess—though this friend used her first name to refer to this person, but we have not felt a need to move beyond this person's role as organizer and hostess of this "party"— has tried, you will notice, to minimize the name and the title you refer to, usually on the invitations relying on a shamrock isolated on a

plain white back-ground... and inside, complicated directions as to the date, time for arriving at the site of this happy occasion.

Indeed, she is fully aware of this dimension
of the party that really if you come to think of
it has a sort of parallel relationship to Labor
Day in September. This friend, refusing to
hold back, adds, I know exactly what she
means by her discomfort with the religious dimension in the same way why would any
woman want to celebrate Labor Day as the
one aspect of that day which is never mentioned: only women swollen with child, go into
labor... can that be said of any man? Even
those men who say they are capable of identi-
fying with a woman usually and in fact always
draw the line at that aspect of their commit-
ment to identification with a woman....

The hostess had the arrival of her son doc-
umented with still camera and video, though
the video has been lost and was only watched
once and was seen to be a bit too "icky" for
all concerned.

The actual photographs are not on the
opening page of the album devoted to the life
of the hostess and the man responsible for

the male substance necessary for the production of the event: which is there captured in full if fading color on page three of what became the first album recording of the lives of the hostess and the male contributor to the making of the child which she once said could be entitled, *and then there were three.*

Sadly, it must be mentioned that *and then there were three* rather abruptly came to an end after a run of two more collections and no other titles were given to what was now referred to as *this is the way it is.*

The hostess was in the present moment aware her brother might just begin talking about a movie by Andy Warhol called *Trash* which was not a film that the hostess would like to see added to the sweep of the party's cultural conversation as it was not a ___________ movie[2].

He could probably be counted on to talk about the actress who had a pillow under the dress as a way to attempt to get welfare

---

2   In the space before the noun the hostess would insert what used to be called her Christian name but she is now required to say her first name... which seems....

from the caseworker who had come to interview her. The actress was what used to be called a man who wore women's clothing. The actress it seems did not get, from what she remembered him saying, the welfare check she wanted as she would not give the caseworker the shoes she was wearing and which the male caseworker had fallen in love with, shoes he said would make his life complete....

Long ago she had given up asking why a person would want to watch such a movie as this only seemed to goad him into telling whichever captive audience he had under his gaze the plot of another movie....

In her own practice of exchanging information about movies watched—many would remember her saying she had seen again for how many years in a row, the movie *Bells of St. Mary* and this had been answered by *Mr. Blandings Builds His Dream House* and even the name Dennis Day might be mentioned and another would add Jack Benny and what is the age of Jack Benny would be asked and the correct answer was always given and does not need to be added to this paragraph except to say that one was always that age if one knew really anything of the world.

But her brother is in the other room and the hostess has begun to feel that she can now enjoy her party or this get-together if you are more comfortable with that.

The wife of the butterfly man is telling her that they have discovered a new hobby and it seems like it will turn into an interesting form of art, if you can accept it... with the implied question, the hostess nods her head in complete agreement and both of them feel no need to go down the road: what is art?

The wife speaks so quickly the hostess, while never ever saying anything about this habit of her friend, always feels she is still at the first sentence of this woman's description, **He** (obviously the butterfly man) **and I have noticed up at the country house, the house seems always to be surrounded with small dead things, if you look closely on the ground....**

The hostess, if asked to describe this conversation, aware of course that this very sentence is a sort of interruption yet at the same instant she *suddenly* remembered—tips of three fingers tapping the right front of her brow—she had not put out the milk for the coffee and there had been two kinds of sugar and three kinds of sugar substitute... so by the time she was back listening to her friend, the phrase, ***dead things***, was heard... at which point the sentence took a turn, which the hostess would be as is said hard pressed to paraphrase so she is recalling exactly the spoken words, as she told her brother who nodded his head later... the parts of dead things which are interesting in themselves... some we have not been able to identify but we are sure they are animal or bird and not growing stuff....

You know what I mean? plant stuff?—we are limiting ourselves for now to dead animal stuff—it is always possible we might move to the plant world of dead stuff but that seems so ordinary, as my husband says about so many butterflies he has to explain at the museum: how many ways can you tell people not all butterflies are supposed to be big orange floppy things?!

I am a little uneasy, the hostess ventures, about your collecting but that doesn't mean you shouldn't do it but that brother of mine, when Lightning died suggested I have it stuffed so it would never be gone. It seems he and the wife of his have a friend out in Arizona who has a daughter who has taken up taxidermy and her first project was to stuff the fox and then the mink stoles this woman had inherited from her grandmother—I don't know if *stole* is the right word—but you remember when women wore just the actual skins of foxes and minks around their neck and you could see the feet and the tails and the heads there dangling... he was saying it was really interesting to see these skins come back to life or at least closer to what they once looked like....

O, no, we are not stuffing dead things... these are dead things but more like pieces of bone and what not....

Do you think we have enough types of sugar substitute? I know some people think one of these substitutes causes cancer, according to some study....

The word *cancer* stopped the wife cold as they say. The hostess did not mean to do this intentionally but she had noticed the word *cancer* was worse than an unexpected **STOP** sign in a small rural place designed to raise money for whatever nonsense those people are getting up to.

No, no, it has nothing to do with that—he likes to find these bones and for some reason there are lots of bones all over the property and no, they are not chicken bones… he thought they might be chicken bones but there are so very few… is that how you say it now, African Americans, living near where we have the Upstate place and while I know not all African Americans like fried chicken and they are not always lining up at the KFC… but you are right, the first impression was that these were just chicken bones—but he is pretty sure they are not and is going on that assumption because it feels right from what he knows about the woods, and who cares anyway, who is going to start a fight about whether chicken bones can be used in a work of art or should you always use say eagle or hawk bones being sure of course these creatures died natural deaths…!

The hostess raises her hand in a form of a compliment for the distinctions being helpfully made by her friend but with a sudden turn of the head she **MUST** right away, deal with another one of those problems, does she have enough different types of sugar substitutes: well, she has had enough of this, people will just have to do and put up with these three... there has to be some limit and I wish people could try to find that some limits are not burdensome but limits, I hope you understand, which won't really get in the way of expressing who they really are, can sometimes be of value if one is very careful....

Yes, she will have to find a way back to those bones but the sudden burst of an OUCH could be heard and responding even before a second OUCH is uttered she is right there in the hallway, by the brother of the man who comes with no name throughout this whole party—that is just the way it is— she will not change her mind—of course, the man who comes with no name contributed his necessary ejaculated stuff for the creation of the child, but here was his brother Stew, short for Stewart—you know, he always thought people spelt it out this way: S-T-E-W-A-R-T though he had insisted that was a mistake, but a common one to be sure as his name was actually S-T-U-A-R-T which came with a sort of British polish (he thought rather interesting, don't you?) though someone replied, rather unkindly it is true, this name really suits him no matter the spelling as he is like a stew that is either under or more usually the case, over-cooked....

Stu (Stew), if we may shorten his name, had contrived it seems to close the door—which he had just opened to make an entrance into the apartment—on his finger, as he closed the door ever so quietly so as to draw no attention to his late arrival, though of course the OUCH annunciated loud enough to be heard *in the two other rooms* above the many monologues being performed and answered in turn by further monologues... there was a near uniform moment of silence which was quickly obliterate in the favor of finishing the enunciated thoughts.

Stew (Stu) could be described as a fixture, familiar in many rooms, but that is sadly all that can be said about his appearance. Just as you are only aware of a toilet paper or soap dispenser when for some reason it is not doing the task it was made for..., Stu (Stew) slipped into and out of these parties usually in a faultless manner except today he had inadvertently drawn attention to his arrival and people—who can be so cruel or so kind—remember he is the youngest of the rabbi's children and has actually finished college within the four years unlike the un-named brother and the sister who both dithered about in the hopes of finding something or other....

Stew (Stu) who was not as adventurous as the un-named brother who made it as far as Illinois where he spent his academic years—or college years—those difficult times he was fond of reminding anyone who might listen and everyone did get a chance to hear at length the complexity of that brother's college years.

On the other hand or foot or finger or ear for that matter, Stu (Stew) went to college to study classical music theory—much in accord with the wishes of his father—but all that was said (by rather gossipy busy-bodies) about this was that he had actually wanted to write off-Broadway musical comedy—an ambition that was revealed once upon a time after a third vodka, easy on the water——and fi-nally found a nitch as it was called composing short pieces of music used in advertisements for the automobile industry.

The Rabbi reluctantly paid the tuition, room and board for this very expensive col-lege in Ohio and Stu (Stew) while not an un-grateful son repaid his father by bringing home a large breasted farm beauty from a neighboring state who had the interesting habit of chewing gum and arguing the finer points of Jewish and Christian theology with a certain intensity as to where they agree and where they went their separate ways as she so interestingly said. This girl concluded after the second abortion she endured that Stu (Stew) was not the marrying kind.

Of course, abortion is a serious matter and upon the death of the rabbi he was hailed by his congregation as a great supporter of a woman's right to choose... about which he would mutter under his breath that his youngest son had been fortunate in this mat-ter of legality....

This girl went on to be a supporter of a woman's right to die and probably in no small way this was a result of her experience with Stew (Stu) who at first had been happy at the possible birth of a child but then thought better of it, *twice*.

This girl, from Ohio, no, this woman from Ohio was rumored to have commented on one of the reasons behind her support for a woman's right to die was that of course she would also support this right for men and would even be interested in trying to evolve a way by which certain men *and* women might be encouraged to avail themselves of this right, even when not under the immediate pain of some life destroying illness, since some people have an almost inherent ability to only sow misery into the lives of the people they meet and even become emotionally involved with.

ENOUGH background. We have Stew (Stu) in the apartment. The heads that turned at his OUCH have returned to their own matters and we want to see Stu (Stew) as he....

Of course. He will be talking about the weather and the traffic on the drive into the

city. There is no need to make a verbatim report of his conversation as it never changes
except once upon a time and which is a family
legend....

So, the weather.

So, the traffic... to both you can supply the
familiar extremes: hot to cold, rain to sun,
heavy to light....

Ah, what is really interesting is how Stew
(Stu) moves about the rooms, always eating
and always drinking something but with eyes
only focused on two areas of human
anatomy. If he looks at a member of the female sex his eyes never go above the collar-
bone and never below where the bellybutton
might be located. If he is looking at a man his
eyes are always focused on an area below
where a belt is buckled. At both sites his eyes
only register bulges of one or should be it
two and one?

Because of the way Stu (Stew) focuses his
eyes he often bumps into things and people
and there is always the possibility of something falling or spilling. The Hostess is ever
alert to these possibilities....

Scattered throughout the apartment are little

piles of towels just in case the resulting sure consequence of both the focused nature of his eyes and the resulting contacts with....

But never with the lack of a sentence of conversation Stu (Stew) slides about the rooms and from one end of the apartment to the other every "guest" is made aware of the nature of his traveling into the city and the condition of the weather he encountered. His presence could be seen as constant and might stand for the range of reactions to the nature of getting to the party and the climatic variability encountered or experienced by every single person there that day. But the observant and remembering participant in these parties is sure also to remember—and while memory can have a way of slowing down the forward momentum of the party—the revelation of Stu's (Stew's) particular vocation must be allowed to shine forth.

As the youngest son of the Rabbi and the one of the three of them who claimed some ability in the field of mathematics due to his interest in music allowed himself to be described as having the knack for managing financial matters. Into his hands fell the estate of the father whose death has not been described as such would cast a possible pall over such a pleasant celebratory event, but the estate was considerable as the Rabbi had, it is said, an ability and a gift for multiplying loaves and fishes as it were into cold hard cash. And while no aspiration is being made to The One described sometimes as a rabbi and claimed as the founder of the Christian religion, Stew's (Stu's) father did share obviously in a modern manner this ability to make money out of something rather simple.

And no, he did not sell any aspects of his religious vocation to such a vulgar end or even one as pleasing as was the action said to be by the rabbi in that other story, that he was only pleasing his mother by multiplying the loaves and fishes or did he only change water into wine for guests at a wedding?

We'll leave this to more knowledgeable religious scholars as we were trying to describe Stew's (Stu's) financial genius which saw a halving of the late father's estate.

The saving in inheritance taxes was considerable, and certain of the unappetizing habits on the parts of the heirs of the Late Rabbi

were curtailed and were without scandal...
though the brother of Stu (Stew) who still
shall not acquire a name was enabled to buy
an apartment further along from the one in
which we are at the moment, sitting, walking,
standing—an apartment then furnished to his
own delight all of which was to accommodate
the young love of his life and who did not
wish to become a parent (though, as the love
of the life of the un-named was a young man,
such could only be achieved by the renting of
a womb and all the rest of that new routine
path in life by which children now in some
situations are provided with either two mom-
mies or two daddies....)

Stew (Stu) can be seen talking with the Butterfly Man about the weather but like the
hostess we are fading a trifle and feel deeply
that we should move right along to another
of "the guests" without in some way giving
offense—though everyone should rest as-
sured they are each valued for the contribution each has made to the success, again this
year—if she may be allowed to speak with the
gift of prophecy and without encouraging
part of the gathering who has moved beyond

traditional religion and medicine and now consults with a certain regularity, stones, the movement of planets, the role of scent in determining sentiment...

****

NOTICE
This book finds itself dedicated to
SHIP OF FOOLS
by Katherine Anne Porter
and
NAKED LUNCH
by William S. Burroughs

(Both books were purchased at a considerable discount during the holiday shopping season of 1962-63 at Korvette's in West Islip, Long Island, New York... but had to await the writing of this romance to see their influence brought into play.)

*****

It has come to the moment in the party that catches the hostess caught between the talking to the people she sees week after week on a particular day of the week that has not changed for years... or is there someone she

had meant to talk with but... she is sure people have left the party... so now she finds herself making welcome the fellow who travels
the long journey down from the seventh
floor. He is elderly, though that is one of
those mean derogatory number-based appel-
lations which this fellow rejects as he is a firm
believer in that you-are-as-young-as-you-feel-
yourself-to-be, and an unkind person—there
are some even at this party who would assert:
a man is as young as what he sticks his penis
into... and it does not matter if the receptacle
for the penis is a person of the male or female gender... drawing the line of course
against four legged creatures for a sense of
decency must be maintained... but while the
hostess has never been aware of the passage
of the years as they march relentlessly across
the faces and upon the bodies of so many of
her guests, she personally does not choose to
talk about intimate relations, and while it
might be accurately surmised that she did en-
dure this activity with the un-named man who
had supplied the necessary material for the
construction of the resulting by-product, the
son....

... There had been a later moment—now best forgotten—though, are not such the real meat and potatoes, when she or was it this un-named person announced across the dinner table: we are at work trying to get my or herself pregnant with a possible brother or sister, as a companion for the spawn of their previous intimate activity... but this process came to a sudden end upon the appearance of the young man who stole the heart of the un-named... while another annoying voice was heard to suggest: that must have either been too easy a job or what sort of mind-altering substance were they all consuming?

No one knows much about this *fellow* (as he will from henceforth be remembered) *from the seventh floor* really, though he did give the son of the hostess a copy of the anthology of poetry he edited and which for some reason—sold in the hundreds of thousands... no one can now recall what it was called and whether the son actually looked into the book yet, this is one of the those needless and heedless questions the brother of the hostess would bring up and with no obvious answer so the only result was that famous maneuver, called changing the conversation to the possibility of a late snow this year... but usually the snows do not come after the day of this holiday as that is the last time the red chilled knee caps of young girls can be seen parading down Fifth Avenue....

The *fellow from the seventh floor* once when this sartorial detail from the parade was described was heard to ask if young men ever walked the parade wearing kilts with resulting exposure of male kneecaps but he was politely reminded that generally speaking he was confusing Celtic peoples... but no one then fell into the trap of trying to separate the Celtic peoples and their peculiar rituals and predilections for "folk clothing."

"This is Garcia Garcia, he is from Mexico and he is a wonderful artist who is about to emerge," said *the fellow from the seventh floor.*

"WELCOME, Welcome to our party, please help yourself," the hostess then turned suddenly, abruptly, not out of impoliteness but there was something really bothering in the kitchen and not having the words, just had to get there as soon as her feet could carry her.

The brother of the hostess saw this verbal transaction and introduced himself to the **fellow from the seventh floor**, by saying, I met you at last year's party. Time flies as it must.

Does time have wings in English? Garcia Garcia asked. **The fellow from the seventh floor** with a voice initially sharp intercepted the possibility of an exchange that had the chance of excluding himself since he was the member not in good standing of a sect that did not much hold with such figments of the religious imagination—by saying this is my... there was a momentary pause... a skipping forward as if it were ended with the question: Have you met Garcia Garcia?

Heads were nodded in the correct urgency as the brother remembered vaguely this young fellow or it might have been another young fellow, such youth are in some way interchangeable, but he would not want to pursue that in a carefully argued line of conversation... and replies, Time usually time doesn't have actual wings in English, only angels have wings....

All young men are angels, the *fellow from the seventh floor* said.

An Irish poet called his young male companions angels, the brother of the hostess said, a man named James Liddy and he always traveled with an entourage of angels when he came from Milwaukee....

They brew angels in Milwaukee? *the fellow* from you know where asked. Is Milwaukee not the beer capital of the United States?

In James's experience he more routinely substituted an "l" for the "r".

Garcia Garcia asked *the fellow* what this was all about.

Gar Gar, I'll explain or show you later... but we should get some drink and food, it's in the other room, I think.

The brother nodded in agreement and watched the couple walk down the hall to the back of the apartment where one could note them again meeting the hostess and she welcoming them again to the party and then continuing on to her mission back now in the front room.

The hostess addressed her brother, Good, good, I see you made the *fellow from the seventh floor* and his friend comfortable....

Gar Gar, you mean? And the hostess affirmed this person's presence had wanted to talk about his art... he was not what one might think though of course he had no intention of trying to explain what he was or was not.... The brother of the hostess of course vaguely remembered talking with this young man, whose name came equipt with a name, Gar Gar, which seemed like a growl transplanted or better translated from a familiar comic strip but in a language remote from the common lingo of the party....

But it's killing me, the brother was thinking and wanting to say what he knew from another source about Gar Gar who, yes, is an artist of found things though he did not find them in the woods—such a soggy bug infested region filled with ugly people who did not wash very much—but rather in the medicine cabinets of people he and *the fellow from the seventh floor* visited in the week on a frequent and yet irregular schedule as at one time *the fellow* had possessed a powerful Rolodex and now had a massive **CONTACTS** section on his various electronic devices which allowed for much liquid socializing and the urgent need to use the toilet where he had discovered, once upon a time a treasure trove—is that how you can say it—a treasure festival of possibility for artistic creation on a profound level of insight into the modern temperature or should I say into the modern climate or is that something that can only be talked about in terms of warming and cooling?

Gar Gar would always with great care open the medicine cabinets and look for the bottles and other containers that seemed to have acquired the patina of age by not having been taken from their places on the various shelves... for a very very long time. He would carefully remove the most agED looking containers as he had been building little boxes in order to display these objects... at the moment he was concerned about whether to disguise the owners of these bottles or should he trust to the reality of people's general forgetfulness since hiding the names was to invite an unnecessary level of inquiry and he had noticed that the society in which he found himself cared really nothing about what was visible but anything or anyone that attempted to disguise or hide itself was immediately the subject of what the **fellow from the seventh floor** called the gotcha culture... it was always a sad long descent from the pop songs of his youth and in particular the one with the lines: *I got you babe...* at which point to Gar Gar's undisguised distaste the **fellow from the seventh floor** would grab Gar Gar's exposed penis and give it a friendly shake.

Recently, Gar Gar was heard telling another young man about this grabbing—which while he minded it—was it really worth making too much of it as the apartment was large, this fellow slept much of the day and the night and was generous with the money scattered about the apartment... the grabbing was annoying BUT the occasional lick of this fellow's tongue to the head of my penis is something I really find pathetic beyond words and just don't know how to discourage it as of late he seems to want to lick more than once a week....

The fellow listening to Gar Gar and coming from a village near to where Gar Gar came from in Mexico replied, in some way you my friend are lucky as I have a man AND A woman who want me to do... am I making myself clear... AND A WOMAN who thinks she is a great beauty.

These Americans, both Gar Gar and his friend were heard to say simultaneously... but his friend went on, I am required to go with them to their house in Southampton... at least you don't have to do that!

Both heads could also be seen nodding in the late afternoon in the window of Julius's....

In these moments away from the party there has been a gathering of momentum of so much to say and so little time and so many people who have to know each other a little better and the **fellow from the seventh floor** is thinking—Gar Gar can see on the screen of his face—the moment of their daily intimacy is almost upon them and so it is time to be making an exit and Gar Gar is not to disappear into the bathroom as there is one two floors up and at the same time we the readers were in Julius' Bar noticing these beautiful leather briefcases arriving attached to hands with carefully manicured fingernails, a detail both the other young man and Gar Gar noticed as they too had neatly trimmed fingernails... Gar Gar had been rebuked rather fiercely by another "friend"—someone from the ancient time before **the fellow from the seventh floor**—please, your fingernails must always be neatly trimmed as there is the possibility of tearing, even when such a finger is coated with lubrication, of the delicate skin of the anal passageway.

HOLD IT please. Were the words that could be heard as the hostess had begun the process of making the record of who had been at the party this year.

Please, one more, just one more. This sentence was repeated a number of times and while the results could not be immediately seen, earlier versions were visible all about and no one could resist the not looking at themselves and pointing....

By this time Gar Gar and his friend had

left and were but a memory, as with the hostess who was heard to say, they were here just
a second ago, when asked, who was that
young man with the intense eyes? by the man
who comes with no name, but as you remember, supplied his part in the making of the
son of the hostess. He was told, he comes
from upstairs, his name slips my mind, just
one of those things.

PLEASE JUST A FEW MORE PICTURES AND I WILL LET YOU ALONE.

All of these parties sail off into a sort of
melancholy of who will be with us at this time
next year but the Butterfly Man is not prepared
to go down that pathway, just yet, as he is in the
midst of describing the antics of the butterflies
that are under his direction at the museum but
his voice changes ever so slightly when he talks
about the antics of the museum's visitors... I
just never know really how to answer a child
who asks, are the butterflies real?

You could, the voice of the best female
friend of the hostess is heard... as I learned in
a course I was taking in New Jersey, it is often

proper to answer a question, in turn, of your guests in the form of question: what is the real?

The Butterfly Man shrugs his shoulder... he was careful to shrug only one shoulder as to shrug both shoulders had been discouraged in the junior high school on the Upper West Side of Manhattan as being a gesture that was experienced as being excessive, condescending and possibly as an un-necessarily hostile response to students who were inevitably not of the ethnic, racial or religious background of a teacher such as the Butterfly Man.

I usually say the butterflies are as real as the nose on your face. It must be understood that the Butterfly Man had once upon a time read a novel by Nathaniel West called ***Miss Lonelyhearts*** and, since he had this book under his belt, as he liked to say, he was always careful to have scanned the audience for anyone who might be missing a nose... if you follow me and if you have read that novel you know about the problem of a missing nose....

Now   ***this is a tricky moment in the course of this party.***

It is necessary to introduce the wife of the brother of the hostess and this is complicated as there are two wives of this man at the party, one current and one of a prior time and the wife of a prior time maintains a friendship with the hostess while the current wife is a little more distant in the scale of such relationships.

The current wife is asking the brother of the hostess, you have given the reader the sense that possibly these butterflies are flying about when in fact they are all under glass spread upon prepared paper and cured in some process to prevent natural deterioration... am I not right?

RIGHT HERE IS THE SURE COMPLEXITY

Neither the brother of the hostess or the current wife has been to the museum to see these creatures, so the reader has had the chance to experience an un-reliable moment of narration.

It seems, upon some sort of investigation, that the museum's visitors or "guests"—as such are now always referred to in public places, hotels, hospitals, jails, subway cars—are taken into some sort of enclosure and allowed to experience butterflies doing what butterflies do, or better in the words of the painter Jack Wesley when asked what the birds he was watching with his binoculars were doing, he replied the birds are doing bird things.

However, no one need be detained by these details as the Butterfly Man has hurried off for dessert seconds and is asking at the same time the hostess if he can help with the clean up... but she is now, does anyone want tea, we have four varieties but one just never knows and there is all this wine that needs to be consumed....

I am doing my share, says Stew (Stu). I hope not too many people will pitch in or should I say drink-in.... Surely you remember when there were all those things that people did to which they added the word, "in"? You know, drive-ins, throw-ins, talk-ins, sit-ins, laugh-ins and need I remind you of the fuck-ins and then the suck-ins?

O, Stewey (Stu) you have your head in the toilet bowl. The person of this voice is

Rivka-Rachel—known to one and all as the sister who comes between him—the man who has no name—and the addressee who turns like a boy caught with his hand in the cookie jar... at which she is raising her hand and covering her mouth with the palm while nodding her head. I don't want to stifle you but your historical excursions are pointless and while not as dumb as your financial expertise can we just move it all along as no one is interested in that sort of history, anymore.

Rivka-Rachel turns on her high heel and walks with her partner Abigal back to the front of the apartment as the temptations of food are too great and Abigal is still smarting from the lousy settlement with that old SOB of her former husband who got most of their weight loss empire... you remember the story... they were one of the first on the scene to make losing weight a "fun proposition" and also very profitable... you remember their slogan which could be seen along Route 3 leading into the Lincoln Tunnel and along the Jersey Turnpike: GIVE US YOUR POUNDS.

GIVE US YOUR POUNDS.

GIVE US YOUR POUNDS. Even at this

late date and even at this party, year after year, that phrase *That S. O. B.* brings a sort of nostalgic element into the gathering and suddenly as if on cue as if on cue could be heard, **GIMME A SCHVARTZE...** of course there was shock at the sound of **SCHVARTZE** but the politically correct sounds were suppressed immediately by the startling appearance of the familiar familial voice, the Rebbetzin had been heard from and even the hostess was quick to the front with: a bit of ice with your scotch?

While it may stretch the bounds of realism and just the thought of such doesn't and can't be happening in this day, but yes, **THE Rebbetzin** has appeared and she is all smiles and hand waving—bright red lipstick a bit smeared at the corners from the brush-by-kisses high-lighted by a last memory that the brother of the hostess has of the appearance of **THE Rebbetzin** in this apartment

—can one say a donkey's years ago... and it was the same command: **GIMME A SCHVARTZE** back in the day, as he has learned to say, he was remembering her saying, I love so much the label with those darling little black and white dogs... and I have always thought the black one was meant for me but the Rebbe did not fancy dogs in the house as he was always complaining they took away from his concentration and they shed hair all over the furniture and it costs a fortune to get the hair and smell out of the cushions....

It should be noted that both the man without a name and his sister Rivka-Rachel, and Stu (Stew). did not seem to notice or even hear the same voice that both the hostess and her brother have heard... but that was always as it was since the Rebbetzin and her husband cherished her and it was said, she is the real child they never had and such a caring hostess not like those closest to me. (Here the Rebbetzin aiming for her right breast with the palm of her hand plants that appendage to an area of the main digestive organ and the wonderful phrase is uttered: I am famished.)

However, this is a party... and such should be curtailed, though one last factual bit: you were probably wondering about that name Rivka-Rachel? Legend has it that both the Rebbe and the wife were so tired of being asked are you a father yet, are you a mother yet... they both agreed on the double name which was shortened to RR or Are-Are and the thanked WHOEVER is appropriate for having a daughter who didn't much like men —as they were afraid that RR might mean she would be like the railroad tracks and too many locomotives might roll over her... so it was and always will be and we are all probably blessed by a simple sadly realistic fact: the Rebbe and his wife are no longer in the world of the so-called living...

(and the serious reader all along has been asking the question: are they here present or are they shades who escaped from under the tiny memorial pile of stones placed upon their tomb-marker? Sorry to say there is no answer to the question.)

... yet the wife of the brother of the hostess is heard to remind him there is the phrase **to get**

on the train but you need seven Afro-American gentlemen in a neat line waiting their turn to make a deposit inside and... though in the multiplicity of apparent narrators someone else could be hearing a sort of descending silence which for a moment will preserve by holding the tongue of this brother as a he begins to prepare to recount again the famous holiday visit of the Rebbe and his wife to this very apartment in that difficult month of December... but we will have to come back to that later as there is a small commotion in the hallway as the toilet is backing up and someone is sending out an **SOS SOS   SOS** ... all to the lifeboats, all to the lifeboats... however the hostess is there in the proverbial jiffy, small mop in hand and nothing to it, really nothing to it... which is answered with a loud shout: O, my babies... and one can see two large bent dark haired bodies reaching to gather up two small four legged creatures which seemed to be dressed in tuxedos....

Otta and Jyll have appeared—always invited but for the first time in years they have been able to make the trip in from the Poconos... at one time Otta had been a frequent visitor to the apartment when she would take care of the son of the hostess, that is, when she was not in St. Vincent's after attempting suicide... these rather frequent incidents in trying to ring down the final curtain that had begun out in Staten Island where she had been the drummer for the first topless punkish band in New York City, sadly a little behind the San Francisco moment which had by the time of **Otta and the Doorsteps'** debut moved on to topless and bottomless bands featuring both men and women—a step Otta could never agree to... but the reasons will have to await their retelling as the feet covered in imitation patent leather booties have become wet and Jyll is on the verge of a scene, possibly waiting to be seen by some of the sudden onlookers who while disapproving of the spectacle of a grown woman rolling on the floor in an incredibly awkward fashion while banging her fists against the bare and increasingly splintering floor, could also approve of Jyll's ability to "get it out"—when she did not get her immediate wish though the hostess being well aware of this was at hand with towels to wipe the bottoms of the wet booties and while wiping she can not help but share with all about, who of course also know what was coming: a number of paragraphs about the recently deceased four legged resident of the apartment whose picture is one of the few which was not a record of the sure decay in its surface along with the sure unstoppable passage of time unlike so many of the humans who were now on the point of total exhaustion at having been exposed to the many photographs documenting their personal histories and the constant appearance of: lines, sag, bloat and all the else the human face is subject to... no matter the goodness of the heart or wherever this thing called goodness might reside.

But a Hurrah! is in order as not a single plate has been broken and with fingers crossed there has been no loss of drinking vessels... but there are those for sure who look forward to the sound of breaking glass so to recount their experience of that sort of music when they were younger though that is not to say we are in anyway not alert to ***the what*** is happening....

Room is made for Otta on the sofa in the front room and the two creatures are positioned one to either side of her while Jyll goes off to the back of the apartment *to look for something,* as she says upon departing.

She is a dear friend, Otta is saying to no one in particular, but I am always concerned when Jyll goes looking as she always does find something or someone and that can be....

No one is listening in the immediate vicinity of Otta and it is strange—to think the obvious—the way the brother of the hostess gives into this cliché as a way of prefacing what is to come next: I wonder if anyone remembers I slept on the sofa where Otta is sitting and while it might be obvious there is one here who probably is remembering certain intimate activities were undertaken and brought to a conclusion that possibly left some need for a re-do... but the wall of taboo hurtles down from the picture of the mother of the hostess and her brother and this picture is saying with a smugness unmatched and impossible to imagine in this day: if I had not married your father I would have been around the world a dozen times... the echoing silence that always accompanied this pronouncement which was issued as if from on high at Furman Lane in Patchogue, at Pleasant Avenue in Menasha, Wisconsin and lastly by Route 9W going north from Saugerties....

However a gigantic door slams and the reader and the various commentators are back within this room of pictures, some of which can be said to be also *talkies* though so contaminated with un-earned sentimentality as in:

look what time has done,

it only seems like yesterday,

we looked so young back then,
however this recital comes to a quick end with the sound of retching not connected to this recital as the person tossing his cookies, blowing lunch, losing it, upchucking, throwing it all up is none other than His Shortness, a friend of the brother of the hostess.

This guy, His Shortness has, over on the Hudson Street, a small kingdom which is notable for a constitutional prohibition against sentimentality, and fond wishes encapsulated in the phrase: it's bound to be better tomorrow!

His Shortness is American but has some sort of connection to Canada but that is lost in the dimness of The White Horse tavern, a once famous bar when bards were preparing their practiced routine of drinking themselves to death.

There is both a play on the family name of the fellow from Hudson Street, and a comic acknowledgment of his failed political ambition: the restoration of boss politics as it once was in New York City, when a man didn't need an Ivy League degree to get a job in the city government... an obscure failed ambition it must be admitted and His Shortness disappears to see if there are any left-overs... I have a hankering, he says suddenly for home cooking that doesn't come out of a box with all those peculiar directions about slitting clear plastic coverings and the waiting for minutes for the cooking of....

Enough, enough the hostess is heard to be chanting as she is well aware the party is in the long approach and sudden descent into Newark International Airport of next year's party which everyone is being prepared to be ready for about the same time next year... isn't that some good news given how everything else seems to be falling down?

As if on cue, one hears an unspeakable thought loudly voiced coursing from the toilet to the right of the entrance and halfway down the hall connecting the front to the back of the apartment.

A distinct male voice—surely not, but yes, it is the man without a name who once contributed the vital necessary matter, inserted in the traditional manner into the vagina of the hostess... not just a shout but a scream of incredible intensity...:

Nature of the scream: imagine:
"*I could have died*"

—a small room, stadium sized loudspeaker.

O, he is at it again, the hostess is saying... at it again... a discreet though decorative screen should be pulled across the doorway so that none might see who was in the bathroom with this man, but we are allowed to understand it was a man... but no one in the room would dare to comment on this detail and in fact even to have this sentence in this report means that someone is, as the saying goes, not getting with the program, **please now, does it matter in the least...** however, no one is willing to join in agreeing because while re-dundancy might be the middle name as well as the defining characteristic of the mental capacity of a number of the party goers, fa-tigue is their more constant partner as they begin the slow shuffle of farewell for another year of anticipating the party....

But   the   eye   glances   to: (______________________________)   who wishes to remain anonymous as she has brought a gift to the brother of the hostess, yet the fellow from the Seventh Floor is heard to ask: who is THAT woman...? or WHAT?

No answers are supplied to his rhetorical questions   as   is   it   not   obvious   that (______________________________) is simply a friend of long standing and while the brother might interject—and for a time the horizontal partner of his desire and her own desire—yet, all of that is long ago in a past once upon a time which would be set to the music of ***Once in the Village of Our Youth***.

However, the brother is tone deaf, and not a willing perpetrator of nostalgia upon demand... though can a story be resisted that   has   this   woman (_________________________) in her younger days appearing in the famous production of *The Threepenny Opera* in which she slid down the leg of Mack the Knife, night after night, and of course both Wednesday and Saturday matinees in the Theatre de Lys, there   on   Christopher   Street   so (_________________________) can be known as a "Real Village Kid," a tiny demographic designation, now in some way seen as being...? **the pause...** *who gives a shit!*

Senile, is the next word being heard as enunciated by (_____) and is the cue for the memory of her father who while being a father in some sense to her was more a resident or performer in the cafeterias of the Village of that era—as a then father either took up residence on a regular basis in a favorite bar if he was so inclined or he was part of what was called the cafeteria set, and I am not talking of school cafeterias, as at one time—does the room suddenly go black/white with a hint of sepia?—cafeterias were places of cheap but as is said nourishing food and where a seat could be rented for the price of a cup of coffee or if one had to, a cup of tea, though there were separate establishments for those who favored that drink... (___)'s dad—how he would have loathed that word, *Dad*—a word he associated with living in the sticks that for him began at 14th Street in Manhattan and swept across the nation to the Pacific Ocean, and was not a word to be uttered in The Village... anyway (___)'s father was a joiner of anything that he associated with the word senile and by that in his curious use of the language were organizations or activities for those otherwise known as Senior Citizens—a loathsome phrase was his definitive comment and he took pleasure in saying he was off to the Senile Citizens Center or going on a trip with the Senile Theatre Goers, Campers, Talkers, Readers... you name it and he joined it and took pleasure in the uncounted free things that were left about up for the grabs and you never knew when these objects would be seen as precious items to be hoarded against one of those times....

Before the loathsome phrase showed up, old folk or the aged with an accent on the last syllable, were always depicted as a guy with a long white beard standing next to the Mrs... in her rocking chair... the little woman of the house who was always baking a pie or knitting a wool coat for the bottle of sherry... (____)'s old man didn't do crafts which was a very positive aspect of this man who gradually she lost contact with but not enough lost if you follow as we used to say in The Village and there was always the woman who claimed to be my mother... she is still around, I know that and will always be around even when I know they got six feet of dirt on top of her casket.

But, shouldn't we get back to the party and looking at the pictures on the walls or is it better to look for a wall that has no illustrations of the life attached to it?

And while not totally relevant—remember? when that was the most dreaded word within the academy—it or you or he or she was not relevant to the mess spread across the intellectual floor upon which people were verbally skating... ***but more to the point*** says the tall blonde young man—who might have stepped into the hostess's apartment from central casting when looking for an angel of... dressed in a black uniform with a lightning insignias on his lapel and somewhere there must be his officer's hat with the skull... you get the drift...? the transgressive, as is now said—in a party such as this—in which this young man... is saying: *the real, the what is the real...* the photographs are real obviously in their way and then the human imitations of the pictures are real in a way... but I am not as sure of that as it seems... as we hear the voice of Madore who has not been heard from....

... where did Madore come from?... when did he get in from Hartford...? the hostess always asks after him as he has been here once upon a time... well, he is here right now and is stating: I feel more and more that I am just a laboratory experiment.

Not in this apartment, not at this party, the hostess says. We have all moved beyond that stage, if I may say so.

I feel like, Madore says, I have slipped by my DISPOSE-BY date or was it my SELL-BY date?

(A Pause)

Madore is saying... he should have been saying... more and more as sentences tumble from his mouth like marbles or raisins or possibly a mixture of the same though still saying: you are making me into an impossible participant of this gathering, and I will not have it!

But he is only present ever so briefly as he arrived late and has to leave early to visit a friend who is the midst of using up the last of his nine lives... and I had missed Bobby— you remember him, such a sweet fellow who saw no danger in multiple *partners* when such were the fashion and who as an artist made boxes he could inhabit but his apartment was not large enough to accommodate more than three of those boxes while he had an ambition to fill the world with boxes that would hold aspects of what he saw as THE LIFE.

Part of his idea of what THE LIFE was included a desire to be fucked in the ass by as many men as possible within a certain span of time.

Multiple screens have fallen down about

this conversation: the hostess is just too busy, she is saying or she said and Madore has gone.

Cut off at the legs, was heard to be said in St Vincent's back not so long ago when Bobby....

Death and St. Vincent's: now that is a real downer, the Butterfly Man is saying, a real downer and we all know about it and that is enough: what a wonderful party and I look forward when once again I can help with the cutting up of the tongue: you won't forget, he says to the hostess—who has taken—is it the third of her last deep breaths as the party is drawing to an end and there have been no disasters: fingers crossed, right you are... but until the last person is gone, one never knows and then the possibility of phone calls: something being lost, a long delayed excuse, a bit too early thank you for the party... but she is glad that St. Vincent's provoked no more comments as that was always a place for an unexpected lurch and always of a complicated situation, a contaminating excursion all too frequently to a surgeon's knife, something unexpected being discovered and never a pot of gold....

And her brother is watching once again as Toshko approaches Beatrice—who has stepped from being the shadow of Dante when she might have been Laura, but that would be too sad to contemplate as she would only have three days to live if she became Laura... but Toshko is asking her if she has places to go as he does and does she want to come along but while Beatrice is touched by his beauty she can see the hole in his pocket and in fact a hole in each of his four pockets into which he keeps shoving what is not to be....

Yet, possibly a momentary note is called for: Beatrice's arrival had not been announced, plus of course, who was and why was, and how did it happen that Toshko had appeared at the party... had the hostess invited him...? but then it is possible her brother upon receiving his invitation decided that since it was not marked: GOOD FOR ONE DESIGNATED AD-MISSION: **NOT-TRANSFERABLE**—he took it, as he often did, as a general call to sur-round himself with mirrors into which he could look and see part of his own life re-flected in familiar faces and Toshko had been one of those faces seen first in Sofia, Bulgaria and then in a gypsy village near Zemun in Serbia and then in a refugee camp in Austria and finally—up until this moment—here in New York City where over the years he had held a number of jobs, the most recent being as a person who was required early in the morning to report to a central New York City Sanitation Department facility where city garbage trucks departed for their daily routes and it was his duty to count the trucks as they left and record the exact time for each one of them... his was a difficult job as he was then free, if such a word could be used, until 4:30PM when he had to return to the garage and count the trucks as they returned from their rounds.

Often the number of A.M. Departures did not match the P.M. Returns and as he said, this was a headache or even a head banger, since trucks could return early from their appointed rounds and others were long delayed and while he was not required to sit in his observation chair for more than 20 minutes past the hour of 6PM he was often aware of what he called "the bad vibes" from his superior and while he was not superstitious he had been raised in a family that believe that it was possible to curse a person by means of certain actions: one of which he remembered—his mother had a falling out with a man who had wanted to take the part of Toshko's departed father, but it turned out that this man was more interested in getting you know what for free and then a dipping into her purse for a few loose leva that might be there... and he had seen her take a photograph of this person, and giving it to Toshko to take it to the out-house.... We will not go too much into such details as to the plumbing of where Toshko had been living in Sofia, **back then,** and take this pin put it into the picture attach the picture to the end of the pole and dip into the stuff down there... you don't have to dip it too deeply as the picture might come off but just enough to smear it with....

Doing as he was told, he brought the picture, and the pole to the porch and his mother contrived to get the picture off the pole and with a tip of the knife she carved the eyes out of the picture... she eased the picture into an envelope and told Toshko to take it later to this man's building and get it into his mailbox.

Once upon a time I tried to suggest that this was not likely in his situation in the Sanitation Department but he would say, YOU DON'T KNOW THESE PEOPLE THE WAY I DO....

So, Toshko heads to the front room which is thinned out—where did all the people go and he meets Anne-Marie who had showed up—how was this?—how did she get into the party? Her visit was not expected... but isn't that the nature of these parties....

Anything to postpone the grim reaper's appearance, the chain of rehearsals that one can be aware of before the final sweep of the....

The hostess has been announcing: not to worry, not to worry: can I give you this bottle to take with you—there's even a plastic bag for it, please take it with you! and who wants and who wants and who wants....

And as in the life, parties come to an end and as in the life... but NO, the life continues: the curtain has not been drawn for the last time because with Anne-Marie appearing, a friend of the hostess's brother... let's attach the most famous comment about this Anne-Marie, made by herself, "My husband back in

Paris couldn't even kill himself: imagine! he decided I didn't want him to come to visit me in New York and so he gets a gun... and what does he do: shoots himself in his own hand... it hurts and it hurts... big deal.

Anne-Marie and Toshko meet each other. It is possible they had met before... but they meet and are an item, as has been said for a number of years... but that takes us too far away from the party.... Anne-Marie had finally left Chosei a Japanese bass player for The Plasmatics... she had enough of his rules... he fucked her on occasion but would refuse to fuck her if she had gained weight... he had fat seeking eyes: in a matter of truth telling: Chosei when he first met Anne-Marie... he could sense she wanted... but he told her right to her face: I don't fuck fat girls and don't tell me you are not fat!

Of course, this made him even more desirable as Anne Marie was used to getting what she wanted... there is a long story about her father being on the Central Committee of the French Communist Party and how he had to seek approval from those higher up in THE PARTY as he wanted to marry a woman of the wrong class. But there is no time for this with the party wrapping up or being wrapped up... but Anne-Marie had been a Maoist when that was one way to rebel but she hadn't really liked the Maoists she met: all talk and no cock, she once said... and so when she asked her father about going to New York and to Columbia University to get an MBA... he agreed to talk to the right person as it was better to have a daughter doing that rather than....

This is a literary flaw seeping into what was to be a thoughtful, gasping, tender... moving... elegant ending of the party....

Within three months, Anne-Marie and Toshko were married and she was telling him to put his welfare case on hold as they were moving to Zurich since she was moving up the corporate ladder at Credit Suisse....

Where did all of this come from? Is it possibly an unwanted bulge as the rooms were becoming empty—though have no fear as we are not to hear ghosts talking and arguing with the previous years: this isn't going to be one of those downbeat truth tilting ends of the story trolling the usual paths of the significant and so letting the gladiator out of the room but not before all hear:

We who are about to die salute you!

Silence was the resonating reply to this Roman kiss off, if one is in the mood to get the party on to being over and what better way than to go back, back, back into the back of the apartment to the tables where a disaster is being noted: the dinner linen which had belonged to the mother of the hostess and had been a wedding present so many years before from her colleagues in the New York office of McCrory stores, one of the once popular chain-store chains.

In moments of such disasters there is nothing unusual in the recitation of a history lesson, but we shall not be hearing all of it today as the hostess is saying: beets, beets... who ever heard of beets at a St. Patrick's Day party!

Who could have brought a jar of gourmet beets: of all such disgusting pretentious objects... gourmet beets in a jar that is designed to spill—this is—it must have been the man without a name who cannot be mentioned and who could never resist the exotic, and against which a traditional Irish

linen table cloth, a cloth made in Ireland itself, is incapable of resisting, falling to such
an assault.

The hostess is seen wrapping the defiled
linen tablecloth in a copy of the *New York
Times*, not very neatly and then the imper-
fectly created package was dropped to the
floor and eased with her right foot under one
of the tables.

There are a number of loose ends or begin-
nings not begun: the brother—could not resist, before leaving the party, his using the
word ***fucking*** and a second word ***sucking*** and
he also failed to resist using the word ***fisting***
and then mentioning *a large can of* **Crisco** appearing as if by magic to recall other parties
rumored to have been attended by the man
without a name... and the sister of this man
without a name is standing armored as it were
by a gray helmet of hair sharply asking, and
you saved nothing warm for late arrivals?

The hostess looked at her with an expression, as was said once upon a time, to be
translated in the colloquial as: who the fuck
are you?

There was a stepping back—and on the part

of both parties—as the party was nearly at its end, for this year and would there be another St. Patrick's Day party next year? The divinity was not called down to reply or echo....

Who knows, was heard and it could only have been the Butterfly Man who had to come back to collect his hat, a faded New York Yankees baseball cap—he would have liked to talk about how he had acquired it, but his wife was downstairs and waited with the necessary patience not of a saint since they were of the Jewish persuasion—non- practicing division... but the hat was essential in the getting home and the hostess had it carefully preserved on the former piano: a man such as the Butterfly Man should not venture into the street head exposed to the sky and had fully resisted the temptation of asking—after that curious adjective: **practicing** followed after by nouns such as Jew, Catholic—can one imagine a practicing Baptist or Buddhist?

So, how to end the party?

Close The Door

and leave the hostess in the apartment by herself.

But that seems unduly sudden, harsh, nasty,

chilly... haunting... desperate... pathetic... wist-
ful... sentimental... realistic and we can begin
to remember or even better invent what happened and did not happen: but the remains of
pictures... no one really wants to know too
much, so we shall postpone more of these
technical problems with the simple mentioning another title:

WHAT ONCE WAS AND NOW...

... always the pictures always a good day and
good food....

Good to spend time with you and you and you and not to forget you

**and the party shall go on for a
thousand years**

(hey, kiddo.... Mimi, here... from the ashes you might say—(laughter please) residing in a container in a closet in Los Angeles... where else would the daughter of a Village kid end up... married to a guy who works in *the industry*—know what I mean... complete with Mom's ashes in a container in a closet......................)

Note from page 11

Privacy at all costs. When, as is expected, Party of P goes into second printing, an ad will be posted in major New York City newspapers announcing an auction to be held and owners of apartments or building west of Fifth Avenue in traditional Greenwich Village will be invited to submit bids to have their apartment or building designated as the site of *Party of Pictures*. Such a designation will add substantial value to said real estate and of course invite additional versions of *Party of Pictures*.

(Clever readers of the first edition of *Party of Pictures* might notice that sometimes 11th Street is occasionally mentioned in the text but this is just a formal fictional requirement avoiding of course the number 13 with its dire fatalistic overtones and 12 with its religious overtones....) Winners of the auction will be able to use any number they wish— courting of course their own versions of controversy.

Thomas McGonigle was born at 110 Willoughby Avenue, Brooklyn, some years ago. His patriotism is divided between: Patchogue, Dublin, Sofia and a base on East First Street in Manhattan. His books: *In Patchogue*, *The Corpse Dream of N. Petkov* (in English and Bulgarian), *Going to Patchogue, Diptych before Dying* (in Bulgarian), *St. Patrick's Day: Another Day in Dublin* and *The Bulgarian Psychiatrist*. Reviews and articles by TM can be read at *The Guardian* (London), *The Washington Post*, *Chicago Tribune*, *The Los Angeles Times*, *Newsday* and *The Hollins Critic*, among others. He can also be read on abcofreading.blogspot.com which he updates regularly.